The Little
Match Girl

First published in 2006 by
Franklin Watts
338 Euston Road
London
NW1 3BH

Franklin Watts Australia
Hachette Children's Books
Level 17/207 Kent Street
Sydney
NSW 2000

Text © Hilary Robinson 2006
Illustration © Sheagh McNicholas 2006

A CIP catalogue record for this book is available
from the British Library.

ISBN 0 7496 6576 9 (hbk)
ISBN 0 7496 6582 3 (pbk)

Series Editor: Jackie Hamley
Series Advisor: Dr Barrie Wade
Series Designer: Peter Scoulding

Printed in China

For Leonora – H.R.

The Little Match Girl

Retold by Hilary Robinson

Illustrated by Shelagh McNicholas

FRANKLIN WATTS
LONDON•SYDNEY

It was a cold
winter evening.

A poor little girl was
trying to earn money
by selling matches.

As the sun set, party lights
lit up in the windows.

The little match girl
huddled behind a wall
to keep warm.

"If I light just one match,"
she said, "I could warm
my frozen feet."

In the flame, the little
match girl saw a warm
fireplace.

But as she tried to warm
her feet, the flame flickered
and went out.

The little match girl struck

another match. In the

flame she saw a feast.

But as she reached for the
food, the flame flickered
and went out.

She struck another match.
This time she found
herself sitting under a
glittering Christmas tree.

As the flame flickered
and went out, the light
from a candle rose up
and became a trail
of a twinkling star.

"That means that someone is dying," thought the little match girl.

Her granny used to say,
"When a star falls, someone
is going to heaven."

The fourth time she lit
a match, she saw her
granny smiling at her.

"Please take me with you,
Granny," she pleaded.
"I miss you."

The next day, as the sun rose, a lifeless body of a little girl lay by the wall.

"Poor girl," said the
passers-by. "She must
have been icy cold."

But the little match girl
was now warm and happy
in a faraway place ...

... where she shone
like starlight.

Leapfrog has been specially designed to fit the requirements of the National Literacy Strategy. It offers real books for beginning readers by top authors and illustrators.

There are 49 Leapfrog stories to choose from:

The Bossy Cockerel
ISBN 0 7496 3828 1

Bill's Baggy Trousers
ISBN 0 7496 3829 X

Mr Spotty's Potty
ISBN 0 7496 3831 1

Little Joe's Big Race
ISBN 0 7496 3832 X

The Little Star
ISBN 0 7496 3833 8

The Cheeky Monkey
ISBN 0 7496 3830 3

Selfish Sophie
ISBN 0 7496 4385 4

Recycled!
ISBN 0 7496 4388 9

Felix on the Move
ISBN 0 7496 4387 0

Pippa and Poppa
ISBN 0 7496 4386 2

Jack's Party
ISBN 0 7496 4389 7

The Best Snowman
ISBN 0 7496 4390 0

Eight Enormous Elephants
ISBN 0 7496 4634 9

Mary and the Fairy
ISBN 0 7496 4633 0

The Crying Princess
ISBN 0 7496 4632 2

Jasper and Jess
ISBN 0 7496 4081 2

The Lazy Scarecrow
ISBN 0 7496 4082 0

The Naughty Puppy
ISBN 0 7496 4383 8

Freddie's Fears
ISBN 0 7496 4382 X

FAIRY TALES
Cinderella
ISBN 0 7496 4228 9

The Three Little Pigs
ISBN 0 7496 4227 0

Jack and the Beanstalk
ISBN 0 7496 4229 7

The Three Billy Goats Gruff
ISBN 0 7496 4226 2

Goldilocks and the Three Bears
ISBN 0 7496 4225 4

Little Red Riding Hood
ISBN 0 7496 4224 6

Rapunzel
ISBN 0 7496 6159 3

Snow White
ISBN 0 7496 6161 5

The Emperor's New Clothes
ISBN 0 7496 6163 1

The Pied Piper of Hamelin
ISBN 0 7496 6164 X

Hansel and Gretel
ISBN 0 7496 6162 3

The Sleeping Beauty
ISBN 0 7496 6160 7

Rumpelstiltskin
ISBN 0 7496 6165 8

The Ugly Duckling
ISBN 0 7496 6166 6

Puss in Boots
ISBN 0 7496 6167 4

The Frog Prince
ISBN 0 7496 6168 2

The Princess and the Pea
ISBN 0 7496 6169 0

Dick Whittington
ISBN 0 7496 6170 4

The Elves and the Shoemaker
ISBN 0 7496 6575 0*
ISBN 0 7496 6581 5

The Little Match Girl
ISBN 0 7496 6576 9*
ISBN 0 7496 6582 3

The Little Mermaid
ISBN 0 7496 6577 7*
ISBN 0 7496 6583 1

The Little Red Hen
ISBN 0 7496 6578 5*
ISBN 0 7496 6585 8

The Nightingale
ISBN 0 7496 6579 3*
ISBN 0 7496 6586 6

Thumbelina
ISBN 0 7496 6580 7*
ISBN 0 7496 6587 4

RHYME TIME
Squeaky Clean
ISBN 0 7496 6588 2*
ISBN 0 7496 6805 9

Craig's Crocodile
ISBN 0 7496 6589 0*
ISBN 0 7496 6806 7

Felicity Floss: Tooth Fairy
ISBN 0 7496 6590 4*
ISBN 0 7496 6807 5

Captain Cool
ISBN 0 7496 6591 2*
ISBN 0 7496 6808 3

Monster Cake
ISBN 0 7496 6592 0*
ISBN 0 7496 6809 1

The Super Trolley Ride
ISBN 0 7496 6593 9*
ISBN 0 7496 6810 5

* hardback